THE MOUSE THAT CANCELLED CHRISTMAS

MADELEINE COOK

& SAMARA HARDY

OXFORD
UNIVERSITY PRESS

One Christmas . . .

when Mouse was just a baby . . .

a HUGE bauble . . .

THE MOUSE THAT CANCELLED CHRISTMAS

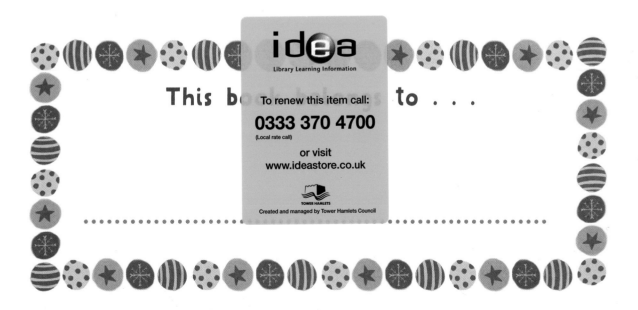

bopped him on the head.

And from that moment on, Christmas for Mouse meant just one thing.

DANGER!

This Christmas, the animals
of Jingle Bell Forest ...

were getting ready to make
it the best **Christmas** ever.
But Mouse ...

was not happy.

'Hold up! Wait a minute!'
he announced in his
busiest, bossiest voice.
'What's going on here?'

'Those snow clouds are getting big!'

He scurried over to Bear.

'Stop right there!' he said. 'ONE. Those pine needles are way too sharp.'

'TWO. These lights are far too bright.'

'And THREE. I hope you're not thinking of putting this very pointy star on top of that very tall tree!'

'Enough snow to make a snow robin!'

'But it's Christmas!' said Bear.

'NO, NO, NO! DANGEROUS, DANGEROUS, DANGEROUS!'

Mouse hurried across to the Rabbit Chorus.
They were singing a song about roasting
chestnuts over a fire.

'Whoa, whoa, whoa!' said Mouse.
'**ONE**. You could have someone's
eye out with that stick.'

'**TWO**. No open fires,
not even in songs.'

'Ooh! Look at those lovely snow-covered peaks!'

'And **THREE**. All that ding-a-ling-ing could hurt someone's ears and it's definitely giving me a headache.'

♫♫ 'But it's Christmas!' sang the Rabbits. ♫♫

'NO, NO, NO! DANGEROUS, DANGEROUS, DANGEROUS!'

'Just heading off to the slopes, back soon!'

Mouse dashed over to Squirrel.
She was icing Christmas cookies.

'Put that bowl down immediately!'
he ordered. '**ONE**. Have you washed
your hands? Think of the germs!'

'**TWO**. That rolling pin
could cause a serious injury.'

ATISHOO!

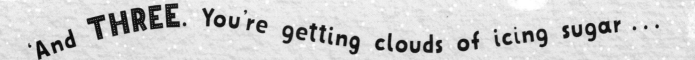

'And **THREE**. You're getting clouds of icing sugar . . .

... EVERYWHERE!'

'No, no, no!' said the animals.
'It's snow, **snow**, **snow!**'

'What's that bump on the mountainside?'

'It's the white Christmas we've been dreaming of. Let's play!'

'DANGEROUS!'

'DANGEROUS!'

'DANGEROUS!'

'If you can't celebrate
Christmas carefully and cautiously,'
said Mouse. 'We won't have it at all.'

'But if **Christmas** is cancelled,' whispered Mole and **Owl**, 'does that mean we can't give you your present?'

'It's a giant snowball!'

'Oh?' said Mouse.
'A present? For me?'

Mouse looked at the faces of all his friends.

'Yes, yes, yes!' they said.
'It's **Christmas!**'

Mouse unwrapped the parcel.
It was a shiny new megaphone.
Just the thing to make a
little voice much bigger.

It was the perfect
present for such
a bossy mouse.

His friends had thought
about what would make
him **really** happy.

'Shhh, Mouse! Your booming voice will set the snowball rolling!'

It was time for Mouse to do the same. He lifted the megaphone.

'RIGHT!'
he boomed.

'Are you all listening?'

The animals looked worried.

'**ONE**. I want our tree sparkling with the brightest lights and the pointiest star.'

'**TWO**. I want everyone unwrapping presents.

And **THREE**. I want cookies, music, and dancing for us all.'

'This is going to be the best Christmas ever in Jingle Bell Forest!' cried Mouse.

And it was ...

but not in the way ...

that anyone ...

was expecting!

'I tried to tell you all
that this would happen!'

Wishing CK a happy Christmas - M.C.

To my parents. For putting up with
my 'creative' mess - S.H.

OXFORD
UNIVERSITY PRESS

Great Clarendon Street, Oxford OX2 6DP
Oxford University Press is a department of the University of Oxford.
It furthers the University's objective of excellence in research, scholarship,
and education by publishing worldwide. Oxford is a registered trade mark
of Oxford University Press in the UK and in certain other countries

First published in 2016

British Library Cataloguing in Publication Data

Data available

ISBN: 978-0-19-274429-6

1 3 5 7 9 10 8 6 4 2

Printed in China

Paper used in the production of this book is a natural,
recyclable product made from wood grown in sustainable forests.
The manufacturing process conforms to the environmental
regulations of the country of origin.

A note for grown-ups

Oxford Owl is a FREE and easy-to-use website packed with support and advice about everything to do with reading.

Informative videos

Hints, tips and fun activities

Top tips from top writers for reading with your child

Help with choosing picture books

For this expert advice and much, much more about how children learn to read and how to keep them reading ...

LOOK
for Oxford Owl
www.oxfordowl.co.uk